USBORNE FIRST READING
Level One

The Three Wishes
Retold by Lesley Sims
Illustrated by Elisa Squillace

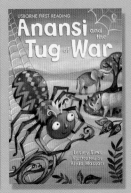
Anansi and the Bag of Wisdom
Retold by Lesley Sims
Illustrated by Alida Massari

Anansi and the Tug of War
Lesley Sims
Illustrated by Alida Massari

King Midas and the Gold
Retold by Alex Frith
Illustrated by Simona Sanfilippo

Old MacDonald had a farm
Illustrated by Ben Mantle

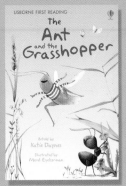
The Ant and the Grasshopper
Retold by Katie Daynes
Illustrated by Merel Eyckerman

The Rabbit's Tale

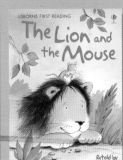
The Lion and the Mouse
Retold by

The Greedy Dog
Retold by Alex Frith
Illustrated by Fabiano di Chiara

How the Whale got his Throat

by Rudyard Kipling

Retold by Anna Milbourne

Illustrated by John Joven

Reading consultant: Alison Kelly

Long ago, Whale
could eat anything —
and he did.

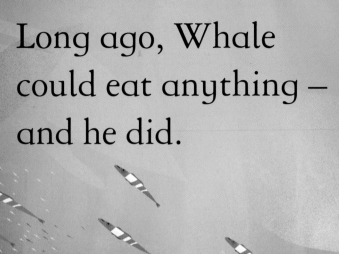

This story tells how
things changed...

Whale was greedy.
He ate crabs.

He ate starfish.

He ate big fish

and small fish.

One clever fish
hid behind his ear.

"Why don't you eat a man?" said the clever fish. "That will fill you up."

"Where can I get a man?" asked Whale.

The clever fish showed him one on a raft.

Whale opened his
great big mouth

and swallowed the
man whole!

Inside Whale's belly,
the man jumped

and bumped

and thumped.

"Come out,"
begged Whale.

"Take me to land first,"
shouted the man.

Whale swam
quickly to land.

Inside Whale, the
man cut up his raft...

...to make a
criss-cross shape.

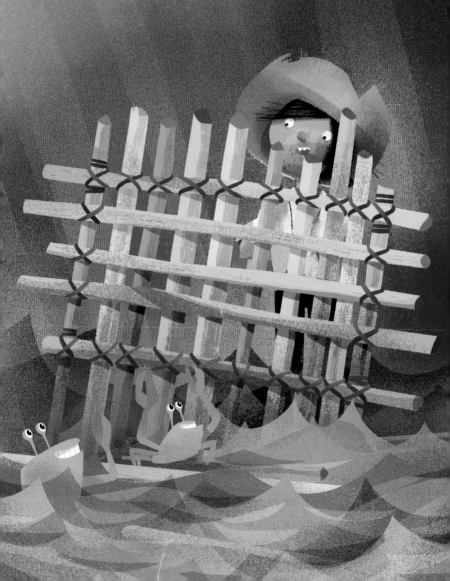

He put it in Whale's
throat.

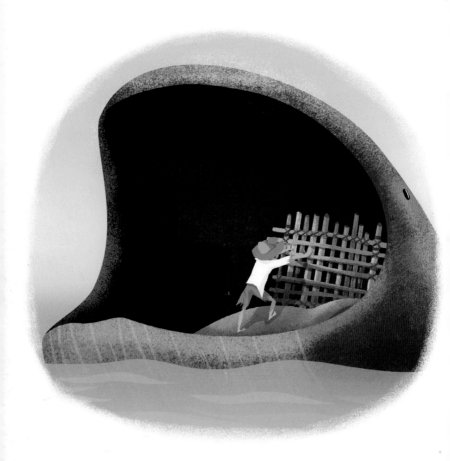

Then he jumped out.

Now Whale can only
swallow tiny things.

He can't be greedy
any more.

About Whales

There are all kinds of whales.
Some, like the one in this
story, have a filter (not really
a raft!).

filter

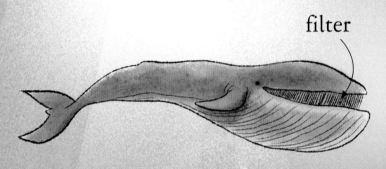

Some just have teeth.

Puzzles

Puzzle 1

Can you spot five differences between these two pictures?

Puzzle 2

Can you put these parts of the story in order?

A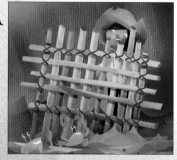
He made a criss-cross shape.

B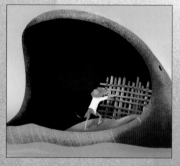
He put it in Whale's throat.

C
He cut up his raft.

Puzzle 3

Choose a word from the box to fill the gap in each sentence.

tiny quickly big loudly

Whale opened his great _____ mouth.

Whale swam _____ to land.

Answers to puzzles

Puzzle 1

Puzzle 2

C

He cut up
his raft.

A

He made a
criss-cross shape.

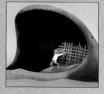
B

He put it in
Whale's throat.

Puzzle 3

Whale opened his
great <u>big</u> mouth.

Whale swam
<u>quickly</u> to land.

Designed by Sam Whibley
Series designer: Russell Punter
Series editor: Lesley Sims
Digital manipulation: Nick Wakeford

First published in 2016 by Usborne Publishing Ltd., Usborne House,
83-85 Saffron Hill, London EC1N 8RT, England. www.usborne.com
Copyright © 2016 Usborne Publishing Ltd.

USBORNE FIRST READING
Level Two

USBORNE FIRST READING

The Magic Melon

Retold by Rosie Dickins
Illustrated by Tara Rojo

USBORNE FIRST READING

Little Miss Muffet

Retold by Russell Punter
Illustrated by Lorena Alvarez

USBORNE FIRST READING

How Bear Lost his Tail

Retold by Lucy Bowman
Illustrated by Ciaran Duffy

USBORNE FIRST READING

Doctor Foster went to Gloucester

Retold by Russell Punter
Illustrated by David Semple

USBORNE FIRST READING

The Christmas Cobwebs

Retold by Lesley Sims
Illustrated by Ben Mantle

USBORNE FIRST READING

Clever Rabbit and the Lion

Illustrated by Daniel

USBORNE FIRST READING

The Dragon and the Phoenix

Retold by Lesley Sims
Illustrated by Graham Philpot

USBORNE FIRST READING

Stone Soup

Retold by Lesley Sims
Illustrated by Georgien Overwater

USBORNE FIRST READING

King Donkey Ears

Retold by Lesley Sims
Illustrated by Mike and Carl Gordon